dark sons

Other books by Nikki Grimes:

A Girl Named Mister

Voices of Christmas

dark sons

Nikki Grimes

ZONDERVAN.com/
AUTHORTRACKER
follow your favorite authors

Acknowledgements

Many thanks to Hebrew Union College of New York for opening the doors of its research library to me.

Thanks to HUC's Rachel D. Miller, assistant to the Dean's Office, for her aid in arranging key interviews. Thanks to Dean Rabbi Aaron Panken and to Dr. David Sperling, professor of Bible and a specialist in Genesis, for allowing me to interview them concerning, among other things, Jewish beliefs and practices during the time of Abraham.

Thanks to Bryan Green, Rebecca Marsh, Sheila Northcutt, Mary Norton, Drew Ward, and Imani Whyte for reading various drafts of the manuscript and for generously sharing their insights.

Special thanks to Michael Cart, editor of *Necessary Noise*, for allowing me to reprint the poems which originally appeared in that anthology under the title "The Throwaway."

Finally, thanks to my editor, Donna Bray, for saying yes when this book was merely an idea.

ZONDERVAN

Dark Sons
Copyright © 2005, 2010 by Nikki Grimes

This title is also available as a Zondervan ebook.
Visit www.zondervan.com/ebooks.

This title is also available in a Zondervan audio edition.
Visit www.zondervan.fm.

Requests for information should be addressed to:

Zondervan, *Grand Rapids, Michigan* 49530

Library of Congress Cataloging-in-Publication Data

Grimes, Nikki.
    Dark sons / Nikki Grimes.
       p. cm.
    Coretta Scott King Honor Book, 2006
    Summary: Alternating poems compare and contrast the conflicted feelings of
Ishmael, son of the Biblical patriarch Abraham, and Sam, a teenager in New York
City, as they try to come to terms with being abandoned by their fathers and with
the love they feel for their younger stepbrothers.
    ISBN 978-0-310-72145-1 (softcover)
      [1. Novels in verse. 2. Fathers and sons—Fiction. 3. Stepbrothers—Fiction.
4. Ishmael (Biblical figure)—Fiction. 5. African Americans—Fiction. 6. Self-perception—
Fiction. 7. New York (N.Y.)—Fiction. 8. Bible—History of Biblical events—Fiction.]
I. Title.
PZ7.5.G75Dar 2010
[Fic]—dc22
                                              2010008903

All Scripture quotations, unless otherwise indicated, are taken from the Holy Bible,
New International Version®, *NIV*®. Copyright © 1973, 1978, 1984 by Biblica, Inc.™ Used by
permission of Zondervan. All rights reserved worldwide.

Any Internet addresses (websites, blogs, etc.) and telephone numbers in this book are
offered as a resource. They are not intended in any way to be or imply an endorsement by
Zondervan, nor does Zondervan vouch for the content of these sites and numbers for the
life of this book.

Cover design: DesignWorks
Cover photography: ©iStockphoto
Interior design & composition: Greg Johnson/Textbook Perfect & Carlos Eluterio Estrada

Printed in the United States of America

12 13 14 15 16 17 18 /DCI/ 23 22 21 20 19 18 17 16 15 14 13 12 11 10 9 8 7 6 5 4 3 2

To John Poysti,
who always wisely answered
my theological questions with
a question of his own:
What does the Bible say?

PROLOGUE

ISHMAEL

He calls himself my father.
So why is he sending me away?
This is the question
I'm tired of asking.
Better to accept what I know:
between my mother and me,
we have a bow, a loaf of bread,
a waterskin, and the clothes
on our backs.
No donkey laden with bags of grain.
No tent to pitch against the rain,
or sun, or swirling dust.
Just lonely desert ahead,
a carpet of sharp rock,
a smattering of trees,
miles of dry weed and briar,
without a settlement in sight.
We can expect a company
of wild goats or sheep,
the few sturdy inhabitants
of this terrain.
Fresh well water is bound to be
the stuff of dreams.

My head hurts from
imagining the worst.
I ignore the tears in my eyes,
pretend my father,
a few feet away,
is already dead,
and take my mother's hand.
"All will be well," I tell her,
sounding as manly
as I can muster
at seventeen,
knowing full well
that our survival
will strictly be
a matter of miracle.

SAM

The moving van

pulls away from the curb,

cutting off my air supply.

My anger a stammer,

I stare through the window

at the guy loading his car

for the move from Brooklyn to Manhattan.

He's supposed to be my dad.

I'm glad he's not waiting

for me to smile and wish him luck.

Like I give a flying—

What is he thinking,

leaving Mom in the first place?

Why does he have to run off?

To start some new family?

With *her*?

Like we aren't good enough,

like I'm not all the son

he'll ever need.

And what about tomorrow?

Child support won't put a dent

in the rent,

and Moms hasn't worked a job

in years.

I don't want to bring on her tears,
so I keep quiet, and when she
comes up to me
and slips an arm around my waist,
I say, "Yo, Mom. Not to worry.
We'll be okay. It's all good."
Sure, I know better.
This city's just waiting
to eat us up alive.

BOOK ONE

FOREIGN COUNTRY

My mother and I face the foreign country
of the desert,
valley of heat and sandstorm,
and the false hope
of juniper and olive tree—
just enough green
to tease the eye.
Behind me, the grassy court
of sheep, cattle, and goats.
Before me, the cry of jackals,
the kingdom of Thief
and his brother, Wolf.
Vultures lick their beaks
while eagles draw my eye
to the bowl of sky,
and the horizon.

Beersheba's wild goats, wild sheep,
and boar remind me
that even her wilderness
is kinder than the Negev beyond.
All sandstone sculpture,
a dance of naked mountains
with occasional crags

where wise Bedouins hide,
the Negev boasts the bones
of luckless travelers
whose waterskins ran dry.
Will Mother and I
even reach this desert's doorway?

My thoughts thrash about
for comfort,
and it is this I hit upon:
the life of the nomad
is in my blood.
My father left his father's house
long before I was born.
For years on end,
his family, servants, and cattle
have wandered
from Haran to Shechem,
from Moreh to Egypt,
from Ai to Bethel, and beyond,
with settlements in between.
Lo! My people are experts
at striking camp,
constantly in search
of new grazing land,

of fresh pasture,
moving ever deeper
into the Promised Land.

I wonder, Father,
did your stomach churn like mine
the first time you stepped
from the safe shadow
of your city's gate?
Of course,
our situations are different.
When Jehovah
called you out of Ur
to conquer Canaan,
you had a choice.

Or did you?

BEGINNINGS

How did I get here
at the edge of the desert,
at the edge of tomorrows
as pale as the sand?
Oh, yes!
I was born.
That's how it all began.

Hammurabi's Code of Laws #146

❧

If a man take a wife and she give this man a maid-servant as wife and she bear him children, and then this maid assume equality with the wife: because she has borne him children her master shall not sell her for money, but he may keep her as a slave, reckoning her among the maid-servants.

SURROGATE

My father was eighty-five,
rugged still, but his hair
was dipped in silver
and so was Sarah's.
She could have played the part
of grandmother,
but her long, lonely years
without a child
made that a cruel joke.
Worse yet, she was pregnant
with the promise of God
to make her husband ancestor
of more children
than there are stars.

A sweet promise,
but slow.
Ten years and counting,
her belly remained empty
as an ancient well.
So she told my father,
"Have a baby with
my servant, Hagar.
Make her Second Wife."
The law made provision
for such things.
The child Hagar had
would be as good as Sarah's.
They all agreed.
It seemed
an acceptable solution,
at the time.

SHOW-OFF

One night. As soon as that,
and I was on my way
into the world,
a feat that seemed
like magic
to Sarah,
who'd tried the trick
for years
and got nothing but tears
for her trouble.
Then comes my mother, a dark beauty,
a young Egyptian,
strutting with the pride
of the pharaohs in her veins,
saying, "Look at me!
I am already with child."

I am told the smack
that nearly cracked
my mother's jaw
could be heard
for miles.

EGYPT BOUND

Her clothing quickly
bundled in a sack,
face still stinging,
my mother ran.
Never mind the murdering sun,
the moonless dark,
the distance, the danger
of strange animals
and robbers.
The way she tells it,
she ran toward Shur,
stumbling into the wilderness,
feet split by thorn
and jagged rock, falling,
parched and breathless
near a spring,
encountering Adonai—
      Adonai! My father's Lord and Master,
      the God she barely knew,
      who spoke to her,
      unlike the several gods
      of Egypt.
"Hagar," he said,
"Return to your mistress

and I will bless your son."
He told her
she would grandmother
more children
than she could count.
She believed him,
and why not?
God never lies.
So she rolled his promises
around in her mind
like rubies,
slipped them in the pocket
of her memory,
and hurried home.

THE NAMING

"The angel of the Lord
gave me your name
that night," Mother said,
"warned me you'd be
more thorn than rose,
that someday
you'd be at odds
with all your kin.
I knew then I'd drown
in tears of grief
over you."
I stuck my tongue out
when she said it and
rolled over on my
sleeping mat.
"He knew you, son,"
she said,
"before you ever were."
I pulled those last warm words
up over me,
snuggled up for the night
and went to sleep.

HALF AND HALF

Half Chaldean.

Half Egyptian.

Half slave.

Half free.

Half loved.

Half hated.

Half blessed.

All me.

SARAH

I was only two or three
when I toddled up to her,
in love with all the world
and wholly oblivious
to rocks in my path.
I fell face-first
and let fall tears
of embarrassment
by the time she rescued me
from the dirt.
"Sweet one, come here," she said,
her smile like sunshine.
She set me on her knee
and bounced me there,
humming a rhythm that
wiped away my tears.
Then my mother appeared.
Sarah choked on song,
scowled, set me roughly
on the ground,
and left me there
wondering why.

POSSESSION

Sarah owns my mother and me,
a truth I'd run away from
if I could.
Sometimes I think
if the camp
were under attack,
or our tent ablaze,
we are the possessions
Sarah would choose
to lose.

THREE TENTS

Three tents:
His, hers, ours,
goatskin fortresses
separated by severed promises,
cultural circumstance,
and yards of useless pride.
Even so,
we are joined together
by one invisible thread:
Blood
red.

MISTAKE

I could hate her
and some days, I do,
this other mother who
planned my birth,
then wished me away.
It troubles me to know
I was her idea.
Is it my fault
my birth mother
got pregnant in a day,
then paraded her swollen belly
past Sarah,
morning, noon, and night?
Sarah shares the blame:
it was she
who burned for a baby,
she who wrote my mother
into this story,
she who gave father permission
to bring me into this world.
And now that I am here,
it is Sarah who lashes me
with every stare,

purses her lips
when I pass,
and spits out
her secret name for me:
Regret.

GOD OF MY FATHER

Lord Jehovah,
this evening
Mother's eyes followed Father
as he strolled alongside Sarah.
I watched Mother rock,
holding herself
in the absence
of other arms.
God of my father,
Most Merciful,
look down on my mother.
Burn her loneliness to ash
and scatter it
with the wind
of your breath.

ABRAHAM

I joined the servants
herding sheep today,
my face half hidden by
my shepherd's hood.
I blended quietly
into their brotherhood
and heard them laugh
behind my father's back.
"He calls himself Abraham now,"
they said, snickering.
"'Father of a multitude.'
Hah! A multitude of one!"

How dare they make fun
of him! Of us!
I wadded up all my anger
and spat.
What do they know?
I heard the words
God spoke to my mother,
the words she handed down
like family treasure:
"I will so greatly
multiply your offspring

that they cannot be counted
for multitude," God said.
I fed on every syllable
with Mother's milk.
God's words are what
I'm made of.
Do I believe?
    We'll see who has
    the last laugh.

MEETING PLACE

One morning,
in Father's ninety-ninth year,
I followed him to a favorite
place of prayer,
beneath an olive tree.
There, he lifted his arms,
pale against dawn's purple curtain,
and cried out his petition.
Then he let God
have His say.
I confess,
I heard only
a rush of wind.
Still, I sensed a presence
heavier than air.
Jehovah hovered there.
I trembled until
the moment passed,
then watched Father
stacking stones—
rocks of remembrance
to mark yet another site
where God answered Father
out loud.

THE COVENANT

Father summoned
every male in camp,
slave and free,
gathered us
around the fire,
face flush from
his latest visit with God.
He explained the Covenant,
and I took from it
what I could.

It was all about promises.
God's promise to be present,
His promise to make of us
kings and nations,
to grow our family
till our numbers
beat the stars.
Promises to give us Canaan.
Promises to be our God
forever.

And it was all about signs,
the signs in our flesh,

one generation following another,
signs that would say
"We are God's,"
signs that would say
"We believe."

THE MARK

I.
This God of ours
always wants something new:
Leave your home,
change your life.
Build this altar,
possess that land.
Give me burnt offerings.
Wait on me.
Believe.
Believe.
Believe.
This time, it's our foreskin,
a bit of man-flesh.
I'm all for showing
loyalty to God,
and I am man enough
to shed tears
and shed blood
for the cause.
Only, tell me,
why is pain required?

II.
Last night, I saw no sleep.
My waking dreams were filled
with heat, and blood, and screams,
familiar as the sound
of my own voice.
I rise and shovel my fear
into the fire.
Eyes half closed,
I creep toward the tent
where hot blades wait.
My hands travel south
of their own accord.
I shield my jewels
one final time,
then duck inside the tent
and disappear.

III.
We are truly joined,
my father and I.
This mark of God
connects us
for all eternity.

Nothing now
can separate
my father
from me.

ACCEPTANCE

Mother says
Sarah's given up the dream
of her body's own son.
She's decided
I'm the one
who bears the promise
of future princes
through Father's line.
"Mark my words,"
says Mother,
"Sarah is ready
to make her peace with you
now."

TEMPORARY LOVE

Sarah's invitation
came as a surprise.
"Dine with us, Ishmael," she said.
"I don't see enough of you these days."
And so, I dared accept.
I stepped into Father's tent,
half again as big as ours,
its goatskin walls busy
with shadows born in the glow
of oil lamps.

At the center of the tent
a low table was spread
with baskets of flatbread,
a bowl of dates, bunches of grapes,
carrots, cucumber, and dill,
and too many dishes to number.
A dizzying mix of cumin,
onion, garlic, and pepper
rose from a circle of tempting sauces
to dip our bread into.
Then, there was that special treat:
roasted calf's meat.

More festive than
the vegetable stews
I'm used to.
The meal made me ponder
whether I was cause
for celebration.

I sat cross-legged and tentative,
wondering at the
strangely friendly woman
seated across from me.
"I baked fig cakes for you,"
she said.
"Hagar tells me
they're your favorite."
The dishes before me
were a fragrant offering
my father's smile encouraged me
to receive.
So I lifted a fig cake to my lips
and settled in
for an evening's pleasure.

TRAVELERS

The midday heat boils me
as if this goatskin tent
were a cooking pot.
Desperate for a blessed breeze,
I stand at the entrance.
And there, beneath a stand of trees
is where I find them: three strangers,
faces bright as sunshine,
traveling toward
the cities of the Plain.
Father runs to greet them
as if they're expected.
Distant cousins, perhaps?
On their way to visit Lot
and other cousins I have yet to meet?
Of the few blood relations
we have scattered abroad,
I've never seen Father bow to any
as he's bowing now.
Who are these men
my father deigns to honor?
I strain, but cannot hear
what words pass between them.

Suddenly, hunger blots out
my curiosity and I duck
back inside my tent
in search of bread.
Later, as darkness gathers,
I find Father
dining with the travelers,
his ear attentive to
proclamations I cannot hear.
Something in me shudders, hoping
time will explain the mystery
of these three,
of the hushed conversation,
of the laughter pealing
from Sarah's tent.

RENEWED PROMISE

Angels
my father called them,
the three men whose visit
marked the moment
Sarah took her love for me
and rolled it
like a threadbare carpet
ready for the heap.
No angels of mine, those three!
"God keeps his promises,"
they told my father.
Soon, Sarah's shriveled body
would bear a son.
Sarah laughed,
but my mother cursed,
worried that the joke
would be
on me.

SMOKE

The faint smell of smoke
wafts into my tent at dawn.
The cooking fires
have long been doused,
so I rise to investigate.
My nose leads me beyond
the familiar oaks,
where I meet Father
trudging back to camp,
upwind of Sodom and Gomorrah.
Even in morning's dim light,
his is clearly not the face of one
who's just been promised
a second son.
He clamps a heavy hand
upon my shoulder,
wet and weary eyes staring
into mine, and intones:
"The cities of the Plain
have been destroyed.
They and all within them
have been eaten by
the angry fires of the Lord."

The hard slap of Father's words
brings tears to my eyes,
where the names of kith and kin
swim to the surface.
"But what of Cousin—"
"Lot has been spared.
He and his family."
I let out a sigh.
"All, save his wife."
Again, I feel a catch in my throat,
but Father waves away
further questions. For now.
"Come," he says.
"We will strike camp
and move on."

PUZZLE

I.
Some day,
I will puzzle out
the tie between those angels
and these tidings:
One promised son,
and two lost cities.
For now, I lay my questions
on the mat beside me.

II.
Sleep is no friend of mine this night.
I close my eyes and sink into
a quicksand of gruesome thoughts:
the rage of flame,
the stink of singed flesh,
the smoke-smothered screams
of a boy.
I shake myself awake,
trembling before my God,
whose judgments can be
irrevocable.

III.

And what are his judgments
concerning me?
Is Mother right?
Is a second son
someone to be feared?
After Sodom and Gomorrah,
this much is clear:
for good or ill,
Jehovah keeps his word.

IV.

A second son will come.
Does that bode good or ill for me?
We will see.

NOMAD

We wave good-bye
to the ancient oaks of Mamre
and head for Gerar,
away from the smoldering ashes
of Sodom and Gomorrah.

We are a roving city
of hooves and feet—
sheep, cattle,
donkeys, camels,
and sorry souls already anxious
to pitch tent again.
Where is Father leading us?
How deep into the Promised Land
must we travel?
I stick to what I know:
I load the donkeys
with waterskins
and cooking pots.
Strap tents and
sleeping mats in place.
I grab a donkey's reins
and fall in
with the caravan.

MISADVENTURE

I never asked where Sarah was
our first weeks in Gerar.
Her absence was something
I could get used to.
But you, Father!
The part you played in this!
Why?
I wish I could forget your lie,
but it is whispered
through the camp
and everybody knows it now:
how, for fear of your life,
you watched the king of Gerar
carry Sarah off to his harem,
having told him
she was your sister.
Even I know
Sarah deserves better.
Why did you let her suffer the worry
of landing in another's bed,
forced into adultery?
Had God not troubled
King Abimelech in a dream,
Sarah would still be there.

You say you care,
but what kind of man
risks his wife
to spare his own life?
Where was your faith then,
coward?
Such words will never
pass my lips, of course,
nor will I press you
for an answer....
But the question itself
cuts me more than you know.

THE LIGHT OF DAY

The rising sun
brings me no warmth,
only a cold reminder
of the ugly secret
I learned yesterday.
I dress quickly,
rejecting the smile
I usually wear
for my father.
"What is wrong, son?"
Mother asks repeatedly
until I surrender.
I spew the disappointing tale,
note Mother's lack of surprise,
and cringe, sensing there must be
even more to know.
But do I want to?

THE GIFT

I.
It happened long before
I was born, Mother told me,
a little before she
was taken from her home.
Famine drove Father into Egypt,
a young Sarah at his side.
She was beautiful then,
and Father feared the Egyptians
would lust for her,
and kill her husband
to free her for themselves.
His fear swelled until
he beat it down like clay
and molded it into
a conspiracy.
"Pretend to be my sister,"
he instructed Sarah.
"The Egyptians
will deal kindly with me
to earn your favor."
And Sarah did so.

"How could such a story
have a twin?" I interrupted.

"And if it did,
how could you know?"
Mother tenderly touched
my cheek.
"Patience, my son,"
she said. "Patience."

II.
As Father predicted,
the Egyptians' eyes
glowed at the sight of Sarah.
They praised her beauty
till Pharaoh himself heard of it
and took her to his house
to be his bride.
He lost his heart to Sarah,
if not his head.
Straightaway, plagues
poured down upon his palace,
and in the midst of them,
he learned the truth.
He called for my father.
"What have you done to me?" he asked.
"Here is your wife. Begone!"
A trembling Sarah packed her things

and left his presence,
this Pharaoh who had loved her.
Shrouded in sadness,
he offered her a living token
of his heart—his daughter.

"I was that gift
he parted with, my son.
That is how I came to be
in this place with your father."

III.
What a twisted story, I thought.
Born of such a history,
I can expect my life to be
anything but easy.

EVENTUALLY

How fortunate for me
to be called Son
instead of Wife.
Among our people,
no bond is holier
than father-son.

For all his appalling lies
concerning Sarah,
I need fear no such subterfuge
from my father.
What man would risk
losing a son?
And so I toss these stories
into the dark tent of my mind
with other things
I don't care to remember.

THE LAW

Simple as sunrise,
The law spells out my place:
I am the oldest son,
firstborn of Abraham.
Yet, not the promised one,
as Sarah now reminds me
countless times a day,
oft repeating the phrase
"When he who is promised comes ..."

FIGHT

Mother slipped into
the tent tonight,
head bowed low enough
for me to wonder why.
She tried to hide
her face, the palm print
a crimson scar
across her cheek.

The latest sting from Sarah.

Why does Mother accept it?
Why doesn't Father take her side?
Instead, he looks away
and wraps his sorrow
in silence.

Hammurabi's Code be damned!
Sarah has no right
to keep punishing Mother
for giving Father his first son.
Tomorrow,
I will tell her so.

PHARAOH'S DAUGHTER

One day, we will meet,
Grandfather,
and I will ask
why you gave my mother away.
Was your love for Sarah
so great?
Was Mother simply something
for her to remember you by?
Mother could have been
an African princess,
with servants of her own.
She could have been First Wife
instead of Second.
"It will be better for her
to be a servant
in your home,"
you told Sarah,
"than a queen
in some other."
Why?
Because Father's God
confounded the priests of Egypt?
Because He cast down plagues
your gods knew nothing of?

Was it Mother's divine protection
you were after?
Her royal robes the price
of the trade?
Tell me, Grandfather,
is hers the "blessed life"
born of your imagination?

FRIENDS

They were close once,
my mother says.
She and Sarah.
Like sisters.
I can't see it.
No tent is large enough
for them to share.
The very air between them
turns rancid
unless they're kept apart.
If they ever loved,
there's been
a change of heart.

SACRIFICE

Yesterday,
we rode our donkeys
far into the desert,
and pitched our goatskin tents
under the map of stars.
Long into the night,
my father regaled me
with the old stories
of Father Adam and Mother Eve,
of Noah and the flood.
The ark rocked me off to sleep.
Come morning,
we built an altar of stone.
I gathered timber
while father prepared a goat
to sacrifice for our sins.
And his.
That Jehovah still received
sacrifices from Father's hand
proved a forgiveness
I might need someday.

With one mercifully swift
jab of blade,

the young goat was ready to go
to God.
We lit the fire
and prayed.

THE GAME

We are both men now,
my father and I,
hunched over a gaming board,
silhouetted by a sunset
deep as pomegranate.
I map out my strategy.
For once, I would like
to beat Father,
and badly.
My eyes study the board,
then move up to the mirror
of Father's face.
Our brows are deeply furrowed,
our jaws set.
Father tugs his beard
and I tug my
smooth chin, wondering when
my reluctant hairs
will finally appear.
But never mind.
Now is the time to focus.
I throw the dice,
grin at the six,
and count out as many pebbles.

I drop one in the first cup
and grind my teeth.
This is war.

STROLL

The cold of the desert night
bites nose and face.
Yet Father leaves the comfort
of his tent
for our evening walk.

"Good evening, Father of Princes,"
he says.
It's his private name for me.
I smile each time he says it,
and every time he says it,
he bows.
My laughter only bends him
lower still.
"Stand up, old man," I say,
"before you hurt yourself."
He straightens up,
stronger than any man I know.
"As you wish, sire," he says.
I shake my head, happy that
Sarah is too far away to hear.
Father of Princes is a name
she would rather save
for her promised son.

It troubles her that God has chosen
to bless me as well.
Are there not blessings enough
to go around?
"What causes your frown, my son?"
asks Father.
I shake off the question
and turn my eyes to the sky.
"Teach me more about astronomy, Father.
No one knows the stars better than
the men of Chaldea."
And before the night is done,
he proves it.

ON THE WAY

Shriveled as she seems,
my second mother
is with child—
proof of miracles!
As her belly rises
my mother's spirits fall.
Even I begin to worry.
Will Mother suffer more
at Sarah's hand?
Will my inheritance be lost?
But I stamp my feet,
and leave my worry
in the dust.
My father loves me
and he will not neglect
his firstborn.

THE RIDE HOME

Father counts down the days
until my brother's arrival.
But I have loved
these years
of him and me, alone
on long walks,
trailing our cattle
as they graze,
or out here in the desert
worshiping our God,
our comfortable silences
neatly divided by two.
It will be years yet
before this new son
joins our company,
and even then,
he cannot steal
my father's love from me.

MEETING ISAAC

One morning,
I duck inside my father's tent,
my body taut as a slingshot,
waiting for my heart
to let fly.
Finally, Father lays him
in my arms,
a warm, wriggling surprise
with eyes bright
as shiny shekels,
eyes that plunge into me,
piercing skin,
delving in between rib cage,
fingering my heart.
My lips part.
I try the word: "Brother,"
then join Isaac
in one
unbelievable
sigh.

CHILD OF PROMISE

Long awaited.

Twice promised.

Heir of Canaan.

Born of Sarah.

Son of miracles.

The one intended.

The son

who is

not me.

BOOK TWO

COUNTDOWN TO NORMAL

I.

Another week goes by
and I begin to believe
in the impossible.
I still see my reflection
in the mirror.
No disappearing act.
Looks like I'll live—
if you can call it that.
Every morning,
I wake up choking,
like there's not enough oxygen
in the universe.
Then it hits me. Again.
How Dad jammed a needle
into the thin roundness
of our family
and let out all the air.
Now there's none left
for breathing.
Bastard.
Sorry, God.
No.
I take that back.
There's no sorry in it.

II.

It's Halloween
and the ghost wandering
these rooms
is my mother.

I went a whole day
without cursing his name.
I suppose
that's some kind of progress.

III.

I've stopped expecting
his shadow in the hallway,
his frame in the doorway,
his "So, what's up, Sam?"
at the dinner table.
I moved the chair
he used to sit in, though.
Can't do jack
about the knife
in my back,
but there's no point
in twisting it.

RESIGNATION

Stiff as steel,
Mom marches through
each week
cold as winter.
I'm dazed
and can't figure out
why she doesn't scream
or shout, or fight for him,
for us.
She could've raised
one hell of a fuss
about his leaving
instead of just
kissing the mat
and staying down
for the count.
I bet she never
loved him at all.

HANNAH

She could be Egyptian.
Do a split screen between
Mom and Nefertiti
and you'll see.
She's bossy as a queen,
I'll tell you that.
Never mind that she's
the size of Little Bo Peep.
By thirteen,
I was scraping six feet
and she could still
keep me in line.
She's tougher than
any man I've met.
I bet Dad's new wife
doesn't even come close.

WHY HER?

Why this twenty-five-year-old
Snow White,
all light eyed
and tousled tresses?
Might as well be blonde
to complete the cliché:
black man breaks
black woman's heart
to marry white witch.
News at eleven.
Please.
At least he could be
original.

SCHOOL DAZE

You try concentrating

on the Cold War

or Dylan Thomas

after *your* dad moves out.

Pretending I don't give a rip

is straining my brain.

But I'm here,

going through the motions.

Gotta get an education,

no matter what.

"Yo, blood,"

says my main brother.

"I hear your pop's

got hisself hooked up

with some Eye-talian mama.

That's cold, man."

Tell me about it.

"Yo, man. I feel you."

J.D. means well, but

feel me?

Not hardly.

MIRACLE BOY

The way the story goes,
for a long time,
it looked like
there would never be
a me.
Moms was pushing forty,
with four miscarriages
deleting her dreams
of having a kid
of her own.
But God must be partial
to lost causes,
'cause Mom prayed
till her knees were rubbed raw,
and here I come,
her brown-eyed wonder,
ripped from heaven, she said,
and screaming like
I wasn't so sure
being born
was a good idea.

ONLY CHILD

She calls me spoiled,
like it's my fault.
But pick any Christmas
and I'll point out
the guilty parties.
Take the first December 25th
I remember.
I close my eyes
and that morning
paints a picture
· on my lids:
Lights frame the bay window
of our Brooklyn brownstone,
the way they do now.
Like stars, they wink
at the snowdrifts
blowing past the pane.
I would've watched longer,
but Mom and Dad remind me
I've got serious work to do.
So, my four-year-old fingers
get busy
ripping wrapping paper
from the tower of presents
stacked under the tree—
all
for
me.

BIRTHDAY

I wonder if Mom remembers
that birthday picnic in Central Park
the summer I turned six.
Her red-relish potato salad,
pepper fried chicken,
homemade carrot cake,
and Jamaican ginger lemonade
were all so mmm, mmm, good,
a squadron of ants
rushed our blanket,
anxious for a nibble.
I scarfed down enough for two,
then ran barefoot
out onto the grass,
my T-shirt a haphazard design
of rubbed-in relish,
cream-cheese icing smears,
and greasy fingerprints
that Mom didn't seem to mind,
for once.
I spun myself dizzy,
collapsed on the ground
in a happy heap,
then spread my arms

like some chocolate snow angel.
Mom and Dad laughed,
at me, I thought.
But when I looked up,
their eyes were on each other.
I smiled and, for a second,
let them be.

A HOOP AND A PRAYER

I've seen Dad meditate

at the foul line,

study the hoop as if

his hopes hung there.

He'll stare seven seconds shy

of eternity, then,

easy as you please,

send the ball sailing

for a sure three-pointer.

Even at ten,

I knew it was

a thing of beauty.

One night,

more tell than show,

he teaches me.

"When you pray,

you dial down every sound

except God's voice

so that you and He

seem to be

the only ones in the room.

The game's the same.

You tunnel in,

lock your lids on

the hoop, alone.

Breathe deep,

memorize the feel

of the ball in your palm,

settle into calm,

then shoot. See?

Give it a try."

I do. And, miraculously,

that ornery, orange sphere

whistles through the hoop.

Swooooop! Sweet Jesus!

I shout, do a jig,

and preen in the floodlight

of my father's smile.

EARLY MEMORIES

We were the first to arrive.
Dad swung the skeleton key
to the choir room where
we met for praise and worship.
We were a mixed bag
of supplicants.
Age was not an issue.
I was skirting seven,
Dad was cruising for cane and walker.
(Okay, so maybe I exaggerate.)
The other men and women
fell somewhere in between.
Dad leaned his elbows
on the table,
cupped his huge hands,
bowed his head, and began:
"Almighty God,
I come humbly before you."
Too eager to wait for the others,
he entered into intimacies
with the Holy Spirit,
pouring his heart out
to the one who
knows him best.
I sat beside him, fascinated
that my father had
a direct line
to God.

THE VISIT

What happened to those
good old days?
I should've asked that
when you "dropped by" last week
for the visit you'd called ahead
to schedule.
You pawed at my bedroom door,
panting for absolution.
"Hypocrite!"
I managed to spit out
before anger tied my tongue.
Inside, though,
my nouns and verbs
were locked and loaded
for a showdown
you were bound to lose:
What gospel is it
where a father
leaves his son?
Show me that one, Dad.
Run me the lines
chapter and verse
since you know them all,
drummed them into me

from the time
I could crawl.
Point out the words
where God says
divorce is no biggie,
that you can dump
your wife and kid
and walk away
and that's okay.
Come on,
Mr. God-Is-My-Rock.
Show me.

SIGNS

Looking to lengthen the distance

between me and home,

I train it to 59th Street,

jet through the subway doors,

and run around Central Park

in no particular direction,

trying to leave my anger in the wind.

What's it get you, anyway,

being mad at God?

"It's not like You listen!"

I scream at him.

My dad's gone,

my mom is a holy mess.

So where does that leave me, huh?

Alone, "Like You care."

Out of air,

I collapse on the new grass,

blind to the explosion of spring green.

I blink up at the Etch A Sketch

of skyscrapers, gray on gray,

just the way I feel.

I rub the wetness from my eyes

and let them rest on the sky.

Then I see it.

A plane passing overhead

trailing a sign that says,

I AM WITH YOU ALWAYS.—MATTHEW 28:20

My heart rate slows.

I close my eyes,

whisper the familiar verse

in its entirety:

"'I am with you always,

even to the end of the age.'"

I let the truth of it in,

feel my thoughts stop spinning,

and calmly head back

to the subway.

SABBATH

I'm up and ready
to do the deed.
I've still got issues with God, sure—
and I plan to keep on going
to His house to tell Him so.
Moms, though,
is another story.
For weeks,
she's rolled over in bed
soon as I poke my head
in her door.
"Yo, Mom.
It's Sunday," I call.
But all she's got to say is,
"And so?"

BEST BUDS

Ten minutes after
the processional,
J.D., Reese, Kiara, and me
are in the basement
warming up our instruments.
Our band is on next week.
My eyes revolve around
this small circle like
a camera lens,
clicking on each friendly face,
saving the image for posterity
as we tune up
for a rousing rendition of
"O, Happy Day."
From where I sit,
it's anything but.
Still, I join in the joy,
grateful that I have these guys
to lean on.

SILENT SHIFT

One morning,

Mom marched into the kitchen

to grind and brew

her magic coffee beans.

She filled a mug

and slapped a book down

on the table before her.

I spied the cover.

When Women Pray.

She caught me with brows raised,

sipped her black coffee

and flashed me a smile,

thin as Saran Wrap,

weak as tea,

but a smile, yo—

the first I'd seen in weeks.

"God and I are talking again,"

she explained.

I nodded. "Cool."

She busied herself

with book and brew,

and I left for school,

quiet inside,

knowing that God

had Mom covered.

DECIDING FACTORS

I bet the June date was circled
on her calendar
five minutes after they met.
And here it is,
one week away—
the day my dad remarries.
He asked me to be
his best man—
like I ever plan
to see him happy
with the woman
who won his attention
in a game Mom and I
never knew
was being played.
I'll stay at home,
given the choice.
Mom nods her assent.
"It's up to you, baby.
Whatever you want to do
is fine by me."
How could she be like that?
Ready to let me stand up
for the man who
struck her down?

CHEF

I brown some ground beef,

crack open a jar of spaghetti sauce,

and toss pasta in a pot to boil.

Making dinner is my gig, now.

Mom spends the week

chained to an eight-hour shift

shuffling file folders.

Then, before hoofing home,

she clocks in at the library

for a quick computer class.

She's on the fast track

to make a decent living

in Dad's absence.

"It's all about the money,"

she keeps telling me.

"The way you're growing, boy,

you're about to eat both of us

out of house and home."

It's a good sell,

but I'm not buying.

I know there's more to it.

The long hours she puts in

leave little time

for tears.

VIDEO SLAVE

I hate it
when customers think
young and *stupid*
are synonymous.
(Forgive me, Father,
but I judge them fools!)
Speak slowly all you want,
the video you asked for
simply isn't here.
It won't magically appear
because you raise your voice.
I have no choice but to abide
the rising decibels.
I grin and bear it all
from ten to four,
'cause it's my summer gig
and I'm hoping to stay on
part-time come the fall.
Times are lean, yo.
I need the green.

FIRST SLEEPOVER

It's weird,

backpacking into "my room,"

a place as alien

as a space station on Mars.

I scan the wall,

where basketball stars

preen from posters handpicked

by Dad's new wife.

"This room is all yours,"

she says.

"Arrange it however you like."

I strike a pose

of nonchalance,

then mutter "Thanks,"

remembering lifelong lessons

of politeness and courtesy.

"Sleep well," she says

and disappears.

I kick my shoes off

to test the mattress

with a 2.5 dive and belly flop.

Eyes squeezed shut,

I order myself to stop

imagining Dad and Rachel

rubbing up on each other

around the corner,

down the hall.

I crawl under the covers,

create a clever mantra

to lull myself to sleep.

(So what if it's a lie?)

This is normal.

This is normal.

This is normal.

CALENDAR

Once a month,

Mom and Dad confer

on the telephone,

which I prefer,

or face-to-face.

This time, the scene

of the crime is our living room.

The two of them divide

the atmosphere,

each dancing in a corner

marked MINE.

Territory is understood.

"James," says Mom.

"Hannah," murmurs Dad.

Politeness practiced,

they quietly discuss

who will get me when.

Then, certain I'm unaware,

they cut their eyes

at one another, as if I,

trapped in the middle,

fail to feel

the nick of the blade.

TWO HOUSES

Trading spaces

makes me dizzy.

Two houses,

two beds,

two dressers,

two closets,

two sets of rooms

and rules,

two sets of parents

who split on

the shoulds and shouldn'ts.

Einstein would have trouble

keeping track.

I lack the finesse, myself,

and so sometimes

I throw my hands up,

go for a walk, and tell

the so-called grown-ups

to work it out.

SATURDAY-NIGHT CONFIDANT

J.D. cranks up the music
loud as is neighborly after 9 P.M.
Kids are dancing all over his living room,
and I'm plastered to the wall, thinking,
Why did I come to this party?
Oh, yeah. I needed an hour or two
on neutral ground,
some place without Rachel,
Dad, and Mom in the mix.
Suddenly, Kiara's next to me.
"What's going on, Keys?"
"Hey, Voice." (We use our band names.)
"I'm cool," I tell her.
"Uh-huh. Let's try that again,"
Kiara says, leaning into me.
"Why're you glued to this corner
when there's a party going on?"
"Nothing. I mean, I'm just feeling
like a time-share:
one week with my mom,
two days with Dad and his wife.
It's making me crazy."
Kiara nods her sympathy.
"I know it's a drag. Remember,

I went through it, too.

But what can you do?

Our parents choose the music,

and we've got to figure out the dance."

"Yeah, I guess," I say.

My shoulders slump

in momentary surrender.

"Well, come on then," says Kiara,

yanking me to my feet.

"Let's see what you can do

on the floor."

How'd she do that?

How'd she make me smile?

GOOD NIGHT, KIARA

What's a little kiss

between friends?

A fire that

burns the world away

and leaves everything

new.

ECHO

Last night, I'm at Dave's,

sweating out Indian summer

with the usual suspects—

my high-school brothers.

My man, J.D., slips up on me

and whispers, "Young blood,

if you ain't careful,

one of these days

when you be crossing the street,

those big-ole pants of yours

are gonna fall down

around your ankles."

I crack a smile, which is precisely

what J.D. is after.

"Man," I tell him,

"you sound just like my mother."

He laughs. "True dat!"

We knock knuckles,

then join our brother Reese,

who's cruising the kitchen

for soda and chips.

"Listen up!" says Pastor Dave.

"Next week,

we start easin' through Ephesians."

"Cool," says J.D.

"A'ight," says Reese.

Me, I got no conversation.

My brain is a rattle

of hard thoughts

about the new woman

in my father's life.

"Dude, why you buggin'?" It's J.D.

He and Reese have me cornered

by the fridge.

Reese wants to know

what's got me all twisted.

I drop my head,

speak low so no one else can hear.

"It's my stepmom, man.

My dad wants me

to give her a chance.

But I can't.

Know what I'm saying?

I want to do what's right, though.

So maybe I could use

an attitude adjustment.

Can you pray for me?"

"Yo, brother," says J.D.,

"all you have to do is ask."

We three huddle there

between stove and fridge,

our Bibles resting on the counter.

"Heavenly Father,"

Reese begins,

"look down on Sam tonight.

He needs you."

I swallow hard,

heart echoing

I do, I do,

and slowly

the miracle of peace

kicks in.

OFF TRACK

The other night,

Dad and I are cruising across

the Brooklyn Bridge,

that steel-and-concrete magic carpet

stretching between home

and the rest of the world,

and I'm thinking,

there are folks on my block

who've never traveled

past Fulton.

But hey, what do I care?

Just back from a Jets game,

I'm good and buttered-up when

pow—Dad hits me with

"How would you feel about

having a brother or sister?"

He asks as if I have a choice.

My voice goes into hiding.

I shrug,

feelings offtrack,

mind racing

to the next station.

We'll be home in a minute.

I wonder if Mom knows

and if the news

left her heart bruised.

"So, what do you think?"

My silence is a trick

that fails to work its magic.

"I think it would've been cool

if you and Mom

had given me a little brother.

Got any other questions?"

Finally, it's Dad's turn

to suffer in silence.

That's what he gets

for asking me

the impossible.

DETAILS

I spy Rachel at the loom,
arched over her creation,
mask of concentration snug
around the eyes.
She's full of surprises:
weaving, quilting bedspreads,
baking bread from scratch.
Last night, she caught me
off guard at dinner
with her quick wit,
pun queen that she is.
I learn quickly to think
before I speak,
not yet ready to have her
turn me into a joke.
She smokes,
which I despise,
but otherwise,
she's not half bad.
Except—oh, yeah!
She bagged my security,
stole my dad,
and in the process,
jimmied the lock
on our love.

PAUSE

The sky is slate
and the world is a cold
and slushy place till
Kiara stops by Video Haven,
sunshine in jeans
and knee-high boots.
"Hey, Keys.
I see you're working hard.
Make sure you stack those videos
in alphabetical order."
I smile as if
it's my invention.
The manager cuts his eyes at me,
so I keep moving.
My part-time shift
runs another hour.
"Catch you later,"
I tell her,
and she blows me a kiss
warm enough to melt
every patch of ice
on the planet.
Gotta watch out
for the sun.

ONE-WEEK-OLD

I stared down at seven pounds
of squirm and wriggle.
At first sight
he looked less like trouble
than a blue-eyed,
brown-skinned wonder.
Half black, half white,
half brother, half—what
were you thinking, Dad?
Bringing a kid into this world
who is guaranteed to be
marooned in the middle
of two cultures,
neither this nor that?
Fat chance he'll have
of fitting in anywhere,
I thought.
Forget who his mother is,
or how he came to be.
"Little man," I whispered,
"you can count on me."

CHARM

Miss Italy oozes charm
sweet as maple syrup,
then tries to buy me off
with homemade pizzas
and hip-hop CDs,
which goes to show
she doesn't know me
at all.
Jazz and R & B
are more my thing.
But, hey,
like I told her yesterday,
I'm just in it for the kid.
He needs a brother
who's a brother.
Get my drift?
Well—*tag!*
I'm it.

CONVERT

For the longest time,

when Mom looked at David,

all she saw was

"That woman's child,"

the one who stole

Dad's time from me.

Then yesterday,

Dad and David came

to pick me up

and, who knows why,

but David made straight for Mom,

doing that stumble-run

kids do when they're learning,

you know?

His mouth, an *O* of joy,

eyes twinkling like

Fourth of July sparklers.

He clamped his arms

round Mom's leg

and wouldn't let go.

Suddenly, she burst out laughing,

finally seeing the David I know:

a bundle of cuteness,

sweet as chocolate,

innocent as morning.

SAM-SAM

That's what David calls me.
Once he gets an idea
in his head,
he's got to try it twice
to make sure
it really works.
"Sam-Sam, come play. Come play."
He tugs at me until I leave
the breakfast table,
my cereal half finished.
I groan, but let him
lead me to his room.
"Zoom-zoom," he says,
hauling his Tonka
from the toy chest.
Together, we roll it
from door to wall to bed.
Next thing I know,
he's scrambling over my head,
and locking his
white-chocolate-chunk legs
around my neck.
"Ride-ride!" he demands.

I can't help but laugh
at the little dude.
"Okay," I say.
"Hold on!"

REWIND

The seasons speed like
time's got somewhere to be,
and David goes from
crawling on pudgy knees,
to rocking back on his heels,
to climbing any chair or cabinet
that gets in his way.
All this in maybe
two split seconds, right?
Or is it that the rest of us
are moving in slo-mo,
like some stop-action scene?
I mean, is this real time,
or reel time?
And if this is a movie,
why can't I just hit rewind?
Maybe pause the parts
I don't understand?
Man! There I go
tripping again.
I must keep God
in stitches.

DAVID

I groan about babysitting,

but truth is,

I enjoy the little sprout.

I take him out to the park,

packed in two pounds of snowsuit,

snuggle with him

on the icy kiddie slide,

then make him chase me

for a sip of hot chocolate.

Two-year-olds are a blast.

When I'm with David

there's no past,

no future,

no emotional tightrope

I'm forced to walk

between Mom and Dad

and his new family.

It's just David and me.

Two brothers rolling in the grass,

laughing ourselves silly.

PRIME TIME

The street corner court
two blocks from home
is easy to find.
Just follow the sound
of a ball pounding the pavement,
and kids trash-talking about
growing up to be like Mike, or Shaq.
The first frost is no match
for their determination,
or mine.
I slip my coat off
and run in place
to shake off the cold.
The sun is setting
and they'll be heading home soon.
Meanwhile I share the court.
I jog the length of it,
dribbling my own ball like
it's a head I want to hammer,
and the face
that's painted on it
is my father's.
Once again, he's broken
his promise to join me

for a game of one-on-one.
But it's two-on-one, now,
a new game altogether,
and my brother
seems to be in the zone.
He's got Dad's attention
in the palm of his hand
and he's running with it
and, next thing I know,
I'm yelling foul.
Only nobody's listening.
Nobody hears.
Where's the dad
I used to know,
the one who always
included me
in his game plan?
What happened
to that man?

BOOK THREE

Hammurabi's Code of Laws #170

If his wife bear sons to a man, or his maid-servant have borne sons, and the father while still living says to the children whom his maid-servant has borne: "My sons," and he count them with the sons of his wife; if then the father dies, then the sons of the wife and the maid-servant shall divide the paternal property in common. The son of the wife is to partition and choose.

TWO MOTHERS

All they talk about
is money,
who will inherit
my father's wealth.
As if there were
a question.
I am the heir,
the one who wins the prize:
the lands, the goats, the sheep.
If Father wishes,
Isaac will secure one half.
So be it.

Like it or not,
we already share
his love.

FIELD TRIP

I stroke my hunter's bow
and stretch the string like memory,
snapping back those happy days,
those sweaty hours spent with Father
outside the camp.
He'd balance a bow, tall as me,
while I proudly swung its smaller twin
between shoulder blades
knobbier than I knew,
and we would trek for miles
in search of prey.

How old was I?
Seven? Ten?
He was Papa then,
and could hardly wait to teach me
the feel of bowstring,
to shape an arrow's tip,
to plant my feet
and grip the bow just so,
to see with nose and ear,
as well as eye.
These were lessons
whispered on the wind.

"Listen, son," he would say.
"If you are still as oak,
you can sense your prey
before it bounds into view."

And so, we two would fill a field
with silence—just us men,
drenched in sunlight,
dripping joy,
patient hunters
whose matching heartbeats
drummed out conversations
only God could share.

ELIEZER

Kind Eliezer,
servant of my father,
joins me more and more,
herding cattle,
shearing sheep,
keeping me company
while I water the animals.
A dutiful partner,
he attempts the impossible:
filling in for my father,
who, it seems,
unmindful of advanced age
or proud position,
prefers to play
with Isaac.

THE WEANING

I.
Lambs are slaughtered
and readied for roasting.
Cooking pots are pressed into service
and loaf after loaf of flatbread
is baked.
I make myself a nuisance,
getting in the way of servants
rushing to prepare the feast.
All this fuss is for Isaac.
He is being weaned today.
When I was weaned,
did Father throw me such a feast?
Was it as big as this?
There I go
asking questions
I don't want to know
the answers to.

II.
At the feast,
I face Isaac with a sneer.
"What are you?" I spit.
"A wretched three-year-old.

Your life gives me no joy."
The boy withdraws,
his smile melting
in the heat of my contempt.
Agitated or no,
I sing and dance to celebrate,
as Father requested.
Sarah tries to wither me
with a stare.
Little do I care,
this heart of mine
already calloused
from wounds inflicted by her
through the years.
I have no tears or love left
for Sarah.

III.
Father lifts his hands to heaven.
"God, Most Faithful,
as always,
You have kept Your word.
Look now with favor upon Isaac,
the Son of Promise,
the one you sent to me

in my old age,
the one from whom nations
will flow.
Lord be praised!"

IV.
Father offers this prayer
for all to hear.
Isaac he calls First Son.
Now I am less.
And what is less than one?
From the corner of my eye
I watch my mother
smother her anger in silence.
Lacking such skill,
I storm out into the night
and cough up my complaint
to the stars.

HOT TALK

Forget bone and sinew.
Sometimes I think
all I'm made of
is anger
with a dash of jealousy
thrown in for taste.
It's a bad stew
any way you stir it.
Do something, Lord,
before I hit full boil.
Before I spoil what's left
of my father and me.

SILENT SOLACE

Our God does not often
invite conversation.
We dare not even
say His name.
Yet He visits my father.
Even Mother has heard His voice.
I know Him
in a quieter way.
When I am angriest,
His is the hand
that calms me,
the one that rests
on my shoulder invisibly,
pressing patience
into my very bones,
letting me know
it is all right
to breathe.

TUG OF WAR

Father's heart was shredded
from the daily tug of war.
Sarah's mean strategies
were loud enough
for me to hear.
"Get rid of them!"
I heard her shout.
"Put that wretched woman
and her son out.
I will not have that boy
sharing your inheritance!"
Her words swirled like
dust in a storm,
smothering the camp.
But Father's sharp distress
dug through to the surface.
"I will not send Ishmael away!
I love my sons,
and Ishmael
is one of them.
He stays."
An icy silence followed.
I shivered a little,

then fell asleep,
snug in the embrace
of my father's love.

REVERSAL

Sooner than I knew,
Sarah would gloat that God
had spoken to Father in the night,
had told him his wife was right,
that He should send us away.
I should have kept
one eye open.
I had not counted on
the danger of dreams.

HOMELESS

This morning
my mother's words
fell like a knife,
splitting my life into
Before and After.
She pushed her way
into my tent
at first light,
breathing fear
or fire—
I'm not sure which.
"Wake up, Ishmael!"
she ordered.
"Pack your things.
We're leaving."
What?
I rubbed my eyes,
but there was
no nightmare
to wake up from.
"Hurry," she said,
as if I could,
or would,
rush to leave
home.

STRAIGHT TALK

El Olam, The Eternal God,
Judge of all the universe,
I plead with lifted hands:
help me understand.
Three days ago,
I drifted off to sleep
on the pillow
of my father's
familiar prayer:
"Lord God,
bless my sons."
For years,
I was the only one
to speak of.
Father's love for me
was not imagined.
So why this madness?
Sending my mother and me
out into the wilderness?
For what sin
have I been judged
unworthy?

HAGAR IN A HURRY

A writ of divorce
clamped tightly in her hand,
and she seems prepared
to gather up flatbread
and waterskins
to leave the only home
she has known
for thirty years.
In an instant!
But why am I surprised?
She ran away once before.
Her very name means "flight."
As for me,
I have as much right to remain
as Isaac!
I will refuse to go.
I will stay and—

After more thought,
I decide not to stay
where I am not wanted.

BABY BROTHER

I will miss Isaac's laughing eyes
as we lie on the ground
locked in a mock battle
of clay hedgehogs.
He always wins,
because I let him.
I confess, I often find myself
wound round the finger
of the little brother
who makes me second best.
But I can do without
those other times
when I remember
he is the Promised One,
and I shove him aside,
my jealousy a stutter
I can't control.
"L-leave me alone!"
I snap, happy when he
toddles off whole,
spared from
the jagged edge of
my twisted love.

ISHMAEL

I burn here in the dust,
my tongue swollen as a fig,
chapped lips curled into
an awful grin.
My name is the joke
I laugh at:
"God heard."
Did he really?
Did he ever?
Look at you, Mother,
trembling,
a bowshot away,
your tears
the only water
for miles.
At least you could
have stayed close
to share them with me.
But then,
why should you be
any different?
Everyone else
has left me alone.

My own father
has thrown me away.
So tell me, God,
are you happy now?

MYSTERY

Then came the water
split from rock,
proof that you're
as good as your word.
Angry or not,
I drink, hoping
you'll enlighten me:
Why this miracle?
Why not change
the heart of Sarah,
bless me with the family
of my dreams?
Then I remember,
You are not a god
of my creation.
Any god I fashioned
would sure as hell
give me what I want.
Instead,
you offer me
a mystery.

BOOK FOUR

CONGREGATING

I kick back in the pew,

let the guest band do its thing.

Moms celebrated New Year's

by staying home today;

Dad and his family are aisles away,

here, he says, to visit his best friend,

the pastor of our congregation.

Or maybe he's here to show off

his new family.

I'm not sure which, but

I've got my own crew.

I sit with the guys

from Youth Group,

scoop up a bulletin,

and scan the weekly schedule

for something new.

A pizza party, maybe,

or a teen trip

to catch the latest tour

by CeCe Winans.

But all I find

are the usual.

Pastor's Breakfast.

Women's Bible Study.

Choir Practice.

And this:

Wed. Prayer Meeting, 7 P.M.

Suddenly, I choke on memories

of evenings farther away

than the moon,

images of kneeling

beside my dad.

I look at him now,

rusty halo slipping off his head.

Yeah. Those days are dead,

those times when I trusted him

to hear the voice of God more clearly

than anyone alive.

SPOILER

Next weekend,

I hop on the subway,

sporting a grin.

In one hour,

Dad and I will be together

and I can give up missing him

for a while.

We're meeting at

the planetarium.

Sure, it's hokey.

But back in the day,

we'd hang out there for hours,

just us men.

So when I roll up

on the entryway

and Rachel's at his side,

I'm beyond mad.

"You blew it, Dad,"

I spit out.

"This was our time.

Our time!"

PIECES OF TIME

He kept his promise,
came to my Valentine's concert,
waved to me from the back pew
as my fingers flew
across the piano,
chasing J.D.'s guitar licks.
Man, I was in the zone!
Until I looked up,
and he was gone.
"I had to hurry home
to tuck David in,"
he tells me the next day.
Like that made it better.
Whatever.

BLAME

It's not David's fault.
It's not David's fault.
Here's the deal, Lord.
I'll keep telling myself that,
if you'll promise to rid me
of those nasty nightmares
where I drop-kick this kid
into the stratosphere.
Deal?

ONE-WAY CONVERSATION

At dinner,

Mom flings a pea across the table.

"No, you didn't," I say,

and fling one back.

We're both cracking up when

the phone rings.

She hands the phone to me,

her smile smothered by shadow,

a solid clue about who's

on the other end.

"Hey, Dad.

Can't. I'm busy.

No. I've seen that film already.

Home's fine.

School is school.

Nothing special.

What do you mean,

you want to talk?

We just did."

So I'm being a wiseass.

So shoot me.

Changing the father-son

status quo wasn't my idea.

He wants to set new terms,

let him sweat.

Yeah, yeah.

I get that I have to forgive him.

Eventually.

"Look, Dad, my food's getting cold.

I gotta go.

Okay. Whatever."

Mom frowns at my eye roll.

I slide the phone into the cradle,

go back to the table

and treat my peas and carrots

like nutrition.

Ain't nobody in the mood

for playing with food again tonight.

THE SIT-DOWN

I wake, aware of
the sudden weight
at the foot of my bed,
familiar as childhood.
Mom's got something
on her mind.
"It's Saturday," I inform her,
voice heavy as a hammer.
"No school."
This rough bit of enlightenment
fails to send her packing.
"We need to talk
about your dad," she says,
and suddenly there's tear gas
in the room.
I roll away from the window,
feel the steel cage
drop down around my heart,
and hide the key.
Get in. I dare ya, I think.
"You and your dad
need to find a way
to be together," she says.
She goes on about how

Dad and I are bound for life,
how we will always
belong to each other,
and I remember how much
I hate it when she's right.
"I think it's up to you, honey,"
she says.
"Find a way to work it out."
She's good.
All that steel, no key,
and Mom still found a way
to get through to me.

ONE WEEK

That's what I decide.
Next time I visit Dad,
I'll stay one week—
the longest we've ever
been under the same roof
since he left us.
Left me.
One week.
Then we'll see.

THE ARRANGEMENT

Before I know it,

Spring break finds me

at my father's.

Not *with* him, yo.

Just dribbling on the same court.

Take yesterday.

Rachel kept to the kitchen;

David toppled Lego towers

on the living-room rug;

Dad squirmed in his easy chair,

clipping through *The New York Times*;

and I commandeered the sofa,

racking up points on my Nintendo.

Being alone together

is one game

we're all getting good at.

ONE LESS MEMORY
TO CALL MY OWN

Tonight, David climbs Dad

like a mountain, then collapses

into the valley of his lap.

"Read to me!" he orders.

Dad flips to the funnies

and reads aloud

in alternating voices.

David misses most

of the punch lines,

but this is a rigged game.

Dad tickles him on the sly

to make him giggle,

the same way he once

tickled me.

They laugh in unison, and when

I can't stand it anymore,

I crank the volume

on the remote control.

I'll use the Yankees

to drown them out all night,

if I have to.

CAN I HELP YOU?

The words KEEP OUT

blast from my bedroom door

to no avail,

'cause there's Rachel,

wrist-deep in my dresser drawer.

"Can I help you?" I ask,

jaw so tight, the hinges squeak.

"Oh, hi!

Thought I'd put away

your boxers and tees.

They're still warm from the dryer."

That's when I notice

the sweep of clean floor

where my pile of dirty clothes

used to be.

I never let her wash

my underwear.

I didn't let her now.

I think, What?

Are you suddenly my mama?

I think, Am I some baby

needs cleaning up after?

I think, Who asked you?

I say, "Next time,

just leave them on my bed.

Please."

"Fine," she says,

her voice telling a different story.

"I always put your father's

clean clothes away.

And David's.

I'm only trying to treat you like

everyone else in the family.

You are part of my family, Sam.

Like it or not."

How about *not*?

I keep this suggestion

to myself.

"Look, Sam, our relationship

is bound to be complicated.

But we can both choose

to make an effort.

I've made that choice.

Have you?"

Rachel's question

hangs in the air,

heavy as truth

and no less aggravating.

ALL THINGS CONSIDERED

Kiara's phone rings.

I say hello and she zings

straight to the point.

"How's it going with your dad?"

What can I say?

He's the desert island

I'm shipwrecked on.

I can almost see her

purse her lips,

part sad, part impatient.

She was there from the beginning,

before *family* meant "fiction,"

back when *father* meant "mine."

So I listen when she tells me

my forty days and nights

are over now.

"Leave the ark, Sam.

Explore the new world."

TRUCE

I found him in the kitchen
brewing up a late-night cup
of decaf.
"Dad, you know that film
you asked me about last week?"
"Yeah," he said,
his bent back to me.
"It's playing over on Fulton."
I waited,
let the idea of truce
mushroom in the silence.
Dad slowly swung around
to see if it was really me
waving the white flag.
Satisfied, he nodded.
"Tomorrow, then."
I nodded back,
my anger no longer
locked and loaded.
Are you getting this, God?
This is me, Sam,
ripping off my bulletproof vest
and hoping for the best.

NEED

May rolls in fast
as a bowling ball,
and all the TV ads remind me
it's almost Mother's Day.
I wander the aisles of my brain,
searching for what's suitable.
I settle on flowers and a dinner out.
I've got the *what*.
Now all I need is the *where*.
I'm touring the yellow pages
when the phone rings.
"Hey, Dad."
"Mother's Day is coming up,"
is the revelation he's called about.
"How much will you need
for her present?
I know it's been a while,
but I always used to hook you up."
"I have it covered," I tell him.
"I have a job now. Remember?"
I don't mean anything by it,
but I can hear the air
escaping his balloon.
"I forgot," he says.

Immediately, my mind jumps to

Well, that's what happens when—

but then I cut off my complaint.

"You know, there was a time when

you needed your old man's money."

I tell him it's cool,

that I appreciate his offer.

Somehow, my words sound shallow.

So I add, "Say, Dad.

I could use a few ideas about the gift."

By the time I say good-bye,

there's a lift in his voice

and in mine.

FAMILY NIGHT

The Steak & Brew
in midtown Manhattan
was definitely a step up
from Mickey D's. It was
the four of us together, though
that burned the day
into the meat of my mind.
Rachel sat across from me
and we managed to smile
at each other.
No daggers in our teeth.
No hidden agenda.
I tickled David's toes
under the table
until the little guy grew green
with laughter.
Dad sopped up the moment
like Grandma's gravy.
"We'd like the dessert menu, please,"
he told the waiter.
But everybody in that booth
knew the evening was
sweet enough already.

Which made me wonder:

When am I gonna

wake up from the dream?

D-DAY

It was too good to refuse,

is what he tells me,

this new job offer

that was "on the table."

He paces my room

spitting out words

fast as a jackhammer,

trying to explain why

he's moving

to the other end

of the country.

"What about me?"

"You'll come for visits,"

he says.

His words grind me

like stone.

He's still here

and I already feel

more alone

than ever.

ADAGIO

I slam my door and
plug in my piano,
dreaming life is music
and all I have to do
to slow it down
until it makes
some kind of sense
is scribble *Adagio*
in the margins.
Hell, what else are dreams
good for?

DADDY'S BOY

I miss my subway stop
for the second time this week.
Can't focus with this
swarm of memories
blinding me.
The old life, the old family,
the old Dad.
From day one,
I crawled in his shadow,
insinuated myself
into the hollow
of his heartbeat,
slid my little-boy feet
into the caverns of his shoes.
Need proof?
Peruse the thousand and one
candid father-son moments
captured by impromptu flashes
of Mom's ever-ready camera.
Yeah, we were quite the pair.
But hell, who cares. Right?
Dad's got a new kid
and he's off to Holly-weird.
So tell me,
whose boy am I now?

ESCAPE

I need a place
to run away to,
but where exactly
would that be?
I'm way past Disney,
and I can't disappear
inside a book.
(Ridiculous tears
ruin my sight,
blurring every other word.)
"Beat it" is the refrain I hear,
so I hit the bricks,
duck in and out
of smoke shops,
lighting up cigars
that make me choke.
I wander the aisles of Safeway,
seeking solace from whatever
the shelves have to offer.
I pound grooves into
the corner basketball court
in a pathetic game of
pass the time.
Mostly, I'm just sick
to my stomach.

DIVINE DISCOURSE

What do you have to say, God?
I mean, you're the one in control.
First, you let my father
leave my mother.
Next, you let him remarry.
Now, you're allowing him to move
three thousand miles away.
So what have you got to say?
I'm asking you
'cause my head's about to spin.
These days, I go to bed
too early for anything
but staring at the ceiling,
counting curses
and muttering, "Why, why, why?"
Then, tonight
I close my eyes and hear
"If your mother and father
forsake you,
I will take you up."
Thanks, God.
It's not the answer
I was hoping for,
but it sure as hell
beats nothing.

CALIFORNIA BOUND

Dad's last moving day
finds me locked in my room,
drenched in summer sweat,
a sizzle of piano keys beneath
my furious fingers.
Too bad my playing doesn't
constitute noise enough
to protect me from the sound
of my mother's pleading.
"You should go and say good-bye,"
she shouts through the door.
"If you don't, you'll be sorry."
I know sorry.
It's what I feel every time
I see loneliness
in my mother's eyes.
But say good-bye?
To him?
No. I don't think so.

LETTING GO

Anger was a life raft,
I supposed.
Why else would I cling
till the nerve ends
in my fingers froze?
Next thing I know,
I'm drowning.
And for what?
Dad's as gone as ever,
still remarried with a kid
who's half my brother;
my mother's still struggling
on her own;
and me?
I'm sinking like stone.
Now, I may be slow,
but I know it's time
to crawl ashore.
Never mind the bloody knees.
Help me out here, God.
Please.
I can't use this anger
anymore.

BAND PRACTICE

The church basement rocks
with the rhythm of guitar licks
and hallelujah riffs
tapped out on the rim
of a drum.
"Give me some bass!"
I call out.
Moody as midnight,
I pound minor keys
on electric piano.
I am here to lose myself
in the music,
to jam with Jesus—
the only one
who hasn't let me down
so far.

BAD CONNECTION

His phone calls taper off.

Is it because

I refuse to take them?

DATE

Last night,

I opened the door for

a Mr. Milner,

some brother Mom said

she met at work.

They were going to a movie.

She'd see me later.

By the time I snapped out of it,

they were halfway

down the block.

Talk about shock.

Guess my mom's

Christmas present to herself is

moving on.

BIRTHDAY

I.

Mom calls me a disaster with

scissor and ribbon,

the way I attack tape and birthday paper

on the kitchen table.

I bungle my way through

gift wrapping a finger painting kit

for David.

The little squirt

turns three next week.

Dad thinks he's all about

fire trucks and building blocks,

but I've seen that kid with a brush.

He'll splatter wet rainbow

on anything standing still.

I wonder if that's how

Romare Bearden started out.

II.

Three years old!

I can hardly believe it.

Got to admit,

he's turned into

a part of me I can't remember

ever being without.
I've memorized his giggle,
learned his pout.
I miss the way
he used to shadow me
to see what I'd do next
so he could try it.
He's a cool little dude,
and no feud with Dad
can erase the corner space
inside me
that kid's painted himself into.

GRACE

The months melt into each other,

and all I feel is numb.

That's some relief, I guess.

I hurt less than before.

Is this what you call

grace, God?

Hey, don't get me wrong.

I'll take it.

FATHERLESS

Prospect Park spits us out
after a long walk that
marched us into an evening
of April mist.
Kiara and I rest on
my brownstone stoop
for a minute,
rocking in the silent comfort
of familiarity.
She squeezes my hand
and suddenly, I shiver,
feeling it.
The hereness of her,
the goneness of my father.
Him being in L.A.
feels more like death
than distance.
But I'm beginning to be
okay with it now.
I'm breathing.
I'm alive.

THANK-YOU CARD

Just in from Video Haven,

my hunger deep and wide

as a subway tunnel,

all I can think about

is food.

I open the manhole cover

of my mouth and start

shoveling chips and

leftover chicken in so fast,

I almost miss it:

the 9 × 11 envelope

tossed on the kitchen counter.

The L.A. postmark

sends my pulse

into overdrive,

and before I know it,

the contents of the envelope

are in my hands.

A finger-smudged painting

of two stick-figure boys,

one taller than the other,

both holding hands.

Good thing Moms
isn't in the room.
I don't want her catching
tears in my eyes.

CLEAN SWEEP

I pull the picture of my father

from the back

of my dresser drawer

and set it out, again.

Righteous or not,

the old bitterness

is only slowing me down.

Forgiveness is something

I need to consider. For me.

I love my dad, yo.

But I can't wish him

into being who I want,

or where.

So, it's like this.

I'm gonna take whatever

he chooses to offer,

and get the rest

of what I need

from somewhere else.

FREE THROW

"Life is a free throw,"
Chris tells me.
"The ball is in your hands."
I call him the Man,
this new guy
in the neighborhood
who hangs out at the court.
He's about
my old man's age.
No stand-in,
but he's solid in a pinch.
You learn to make do.
It's no cinch though,
so I keep prayed up
and promise myself,
when I have a kid,
I'll rip "good-bye"
right out of my vocabulary.
I still don't get why
Dad moved away,
but, hey, that's his thing.
I've got my own ball to bounce,
my own shots to take.
It's me standing at
the free-throw line now.

EPILOGUE

ISHMAEL: FAST FORWARD

Here I stand with Isaac,
my brother,
side by side
at the grave of a father
who split our blessings
yet blessed us both
in the end.
And what was there for me, Lord,
all the years between
then and now,
except the memory
of Your vow
to make me great,
to give me princes,
to stand at my shoulder?
I suppose this was your way
of letting me know
survival was never
in question?
Even so, a promise
is cold comfort
for a lonely son
spitting curses by the fire.

Yet, you were present,
whispering sweet promises
in my mother's ear,
coaxing me to flex my bow,
checking the progress
of each arrow,
guiding me in the hunt,
looking out for me
as only a parent would,
being the one father
I could count on.

SAM: DARK SONS

I never really noticed
him before,
guzzling miracle water
in the pages
of that first book.
Then one morning,
my daily devotions
took me to Genesis.
I scanned the story of Abraham,
and heard a voice
deep inside of me.
Slow down, it said.
Take a closer look.
And there he was—Ishmael,
someone a lot like me.
A guy whose father
ripped his heart out too.
Me and you, Ishmael,
we're brothers,
two dark sons,
the spawn of
kick-butt mothers,
adopted sons of a Father
who hears.

It's all good.
You made it
in the end
and so will I.

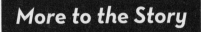

More to the Story

dark sons

An interview with Nikki Grimes

Discussion questions for *Dark Sons*

An excerpt from Nikki Grimes' new novel,
A Girl Named Mister

Interview with Nikki Grimes

What first drew you to the story of Ishmael and Sam?

What drew me to this story was the story of Ishmael itself. Whenever I came across it in the Bible, it felt so contemporary to me. The issues of sibling rivalry, strained relations with a stepmother- or stepmother-figure, the complex dynamics of father – son relationships, or the lack thereof — these are all issues that many contemporary young men are facing. There is nothing dated about the story of Ishmael. It seemed fresh to me, and hopeful. I love that it ends with Ishmael and his brother coming together to bury their father. The implication we get is that they have, through the years, resolved their issues and restored their relationship as brothers. We also sense that Ishmael has forgiven his father, so the story ends on a hopeful note, and I always look for that in the stories I decide to tell — or retell, as the case may be.

How did you decide to intertwine the story of a contemporary son with a biblical one?

Originally, this novel was simply going to be the story of Ishmael. However, after the first draft was complete, I kept thinking that this story was so contemporary it would be interesting to create a parallel tale of a boy the same age living today. I tried writing the story both ways, then gave it to a then-seventeen-year-old to read. He was sold on the version with both boys, so I went with that. I was leaning in that direction in any case, but his unequivocal response was the deciding factor for me.

Describe the research you had to do to bring Ishmael's story in particular to light.

The research was multilayered. I studied maps of the Old World, studied the lives of Abraham, Sarah, Ishmael, Isaac, and Hagar as they all overlapped. I studied the topography of the region and delved into the life and times of Abraham, from the homes people lived in to the clothes they wore and the food they ate. I also interviewed Genesis scholars at Hebrew University in New York and made copious use of their research libraries. There are so many aspects to bringing to life a story from another time and place, the research can be daunting. Sometimes you have to read hundreds of pages of a text to find one useful nugget of information in a single paragraph. When the story comes together, though, it is worth all the work.

You depict a relationship with God as tumultuous at times. Why did you want to show this struggle to young readers?

All relationships are dynamic, and that includes our relationship with God. There is nothing wrong with that. Every relationship has its struggles. God invites us to be honest with him about our struggles, to voice our frustrations, even our anger. He is God. He can take it! It's important for us to know that so that we can maintain a vibrant, authentic relationship with him. To pretend that our relationship with God is all tea and roses would be disingenuous, and young readers deserve better.

What do you hope young adults take away from the story of Ishmael and Sam?

I hope young readers leave the pages of *Dark Sons* realizing that no matter how challenging the struggles they face in life, faith in a loving God can help to see them through. That certainly is the story of my life.

Besides writing, how do you express yourself?

In addition to writing, I enjoy a variety of textile arts: knitting, card- and bookmaking, and making beaded jewelry. I also have a passion for photography and painting watercolors. We all have a natural impulse to create, and I find that creating art enriches my life. Try it!

Discussion Guide for *Dark Sons*

1. What is Ishmael's immediate problem? What is Sam's? How would you feel if you were Sam and/or Ishmael?

2. How are Sam and Ishmael's situations parallel? How are they different?

3. Discuss how Ishmael's birth seemed a blessing to one woman and an insult to another. Who do you mostly feel sorry for: Hagar or Sarah? Why? How did the law complicate these relationships?

4. Why do you think Sarah finally tries to accept Ishmael into the family? Compare his father's home to his own with his mother. How does Sarah try to make him feel welcome? How do we make others feel welcome in our own families?

5. "No bond is holier/than father-son." Do you agree? Do you think this statement is true today? What bonds are truly holy? Why?

6. Whose choices are most difficult to accept in Ishmael's story? How is Ishmael stuck with the consequences of so many other people's decisions? Are all children subject to other's choices?

7. Despite the fact that baby Isaac, the promised one, may split his inheritance, how does Ishmael feel toward his brother? Would you have such generosity of spirit or not?

8. How is Sam coping with his father's abandonment of the family? What questions does Sam ask about his mother? Where does he place the blame?

9. Do you think Sam's religious upbringing makes his father's betrayal easier or more difficult to bear? Why?

10. If you had to describe Sam's feelings in one word, what would it be? Is he justified in his feelings? Is there any positive way to channel all this negative emotion?

11. Describe the difference in the way Ishmael and his brother, Isaac, are treated by their father. Is this fair? Are there always differences between how parents raise siblings? Why do you think so or not?

12. How does Ishmael's life become a tug of war? How would you feel in his world? Ishmael decides "not to stay/where I am not wanted." Would you come to the same decision?

13. Ishmael thought he was safe in his father's love and protection, but he is guided to a new decision based on a dream from God. How would you feel if this happened to you? Would it make you question your faith?

14. Sam once trusted his father "to hear the voice of God more clearly/than anyone else." Could there be anything positive about Sam losing this trust? Have you ever lost faith in a person? What did it teach you?

15. Sam's mother encourages him to rebuild his relationship with his father. How hard do you think this was for her to do?

16. What new decision erases all the progress that Sam and his dad have made over the last couple of years? How does Sam deal with his disappointment and pain? What do you do with your own disappointment?

17. Despite his feelings for his dad, how does Sam feel about David? How does he show this? How is it rewarded?

18. In the end, Sam realizes he has "my own ball to bounce/my own shots to take./It's me standing at/the free-throw line now." What does this mean for his life? What promises has he made himself? What promises have you made for yourself?

19. How does Ishmael's story give Sam strength and hope? Whose stories (biblically or otherwise) inspire your own?

20. What have you learned by reading this story? What will you carry with you?

This guide was created by Tracie Vaughn Zimmer, a children's author and literacy specialist. Visit her website to find hundreds of guides like this one.

**Enjoy this excerpt from Nikki Grimes'
novel A Girl Named Mister**

Mary: When Gabriel Comes

I.
A bright light turns the night
of my chamber into day
and pries my eyes open.
What do I see?
A being lit from within,
a giant whose voice
is quiet thunder.
"Fear not," he says, too late.
I quake, rubbing my eyes
anxious to wake
from this dream.
"I am Gabriel,"
says the voice, more soothing now.
"I bring a message from God."
Trembling, I rise
ready to listen.
Still, what am I to make
of his amazing words?
That I, a virgin,
am to be mother of Messiah?

II.
All things are possible
with God.
The truth of it
falls on me like rain.
I slowly drink it in,
then lift my arms,
surrendered.

"I am yours, Lord.
Do with me as you will."
He wraps his light
around me.

I am never the same again.

Mister: First Touch

How did it happen?
I told myself
it's only touching.
I told myself
my clothes are still on.
But who was I kidding?
Even through
my rayon-cotton blend
his touch
burned the world away.

A Girl Named Mister

Blame it on my mother.
She's the one who named me
Mary Rudine.
The name is some throwback
her old-fashioned thinking
came up with.
Nobody but Mom
has called me Mary Rudine
since forever.
First it was Mary,
then it was M.R.
Mister is all anybody
calls me now.

My boyfriend used to think
it was cute,
a girl named Mister.
Used to think I was cute.
Used to be my boyfriend
what feels like
a million years ago.
Then again, I used to be
a good Christian girl,
the kind who would never, well ...
Just goes to show
how little people know.
Even I was surprised by me.
Now, I close my eyes
hoping to see
exactly where I went wrong.

When It Was Good

Was it that long ago?
I remember one morning
sitting in church,
keeping my eyes on Dante,
the cutest boy in the band.
Mom caught me.
"Quit eyeing that guitarist
like candy," she whispered.
I laughed easy.
In those days,
Mom and me,
we could talk
about anything.

Temple of My Redeemer

A second home,
as familiar as skin.
Crammed inside its walls
memories of
Sunday school,
all-church picnics,
and vacation Bible school
Sword drills.
My youth group meets there,
and choir, of course.
Even my old Girl Scout troop
once hung out
on holy ground,
meeting in
the church basement.
I could always
count on the deacons
to take dozens of cookies
off my hands.
I'm just saying,
God's house
was cozy territory,
no question.
Until this last year.
Don't ask me why,
but something in me
started pulling away.

Choir

For as long as I can remember,
I have loved to sing in the choir.
"Sing, Mister" folks call out
as my voice does a high-wire
reaching for heaven's hem.
I don't know what my friend Sethany
concentrates on,
but whenever she sings
about the Lord
her face gets this inside-out glow.
That's all I know.

A Girl Named Mister

Nikki Grimes

Mary Rudine, called Mister by almost everyone, has attended church and sung in the choir for as long as she can remember. But then she meets Trey. His long lashes and smooth words make her question what she knows is right, and one mistake leaves her hiding a growing secret.

Another Mary is preparing for her upcoming wedding and has done everything according to Jewish law. So when an angel appears one night and tells her that she—a virgin—will give birth, Mary can't help but feel confused, and soon finds herself struggling with the greatest blessing the world will ever know.

Feeling abandoned, Mister is drawn to Mary's story, and together both young women discover the depth of God's love and the mysteries of his divine plan.

Available in stores and online!

Share Your Thoughts

With the Author: Your comments will be forwarded to the author when you send them to *zauthor@zondervan.com*.

With Zondervan: Submit your review of this book by writing to *zreview@zondervan.com*.

Free Online Resources at
www.zondervan.com

Zondervan AuthorTracker: Be notified whenever your favorite authors publish new books, go on tour, or post an update about what's happening in their lives at www.zondervan.com/authortracker.

Daily Bible Verses and Devotions: Enrich your life with daily Bible verses or devotions that help you start every morning focused on God. Visit www.zondervan.com/newsletters.

Free Email Publications: Sign up for newsletters on Christian living, academic resources, church ministry, fiction, children's resources, and more. Visit www.zondervan.com/newsletters.

Zondervan Bible Search: Find and compare Bible passages in a variety of translations at www.zondervanbiblesearch.com.

Other Benefits: Register yourself to receive online benefits like coupons and special offers, or to participate in research.